KNUFFLE BUNNY

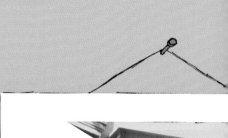

ISBN 0-439-80198-2

Text and illustrations copyright © 2004 by Mo Willems. All rights reserved.
Published by Scholastic Inc., 557 Broadway, New York, NY 10012, by arrangement with
Hyperion Books for Children, an imprint of Disney Children's Book Group, LLC. SCHOLASTIC
and associated logos are trademarks and/or registered trademarks of Scholastic Inc.

12 11 10 9 8 7 6 5 4 3 2 1   5 6 7 8 9 10/0

Printed in the U.S.A.   08

First Scholastic printing, September 2005

The images in this book are a melding of hand-drawn ink sketches and digital photography
in a computer (where the sketches were colored and shaded, the photographs given their
sepia tone, and sundry air conditioners, garbage cans, and industrial debris expunged).

KNUFFLE BUNNY

A CAUTIONARY TALE BY Mo Willems

SCHOLASTIC INC. New York Toronto London Auckland Sydney Mexico City New Delhi Hong Kong Buenos Aires

Not so long ago, before she could even speak words, Trixie went on an errand with her daddy....

Trixie and her daddy went down the block,

past the school,

and into the Laundromat.

Trixie helped her daddy put the laundry into the machine.

She even got to
put the money
into the machine.

Then they left.

But a block
or so later . . .

Trixie **realized**

something.

Trixie turned to her daddy and said,

"Now, please don't get fussy,"
said her daddy.

Well, she had no choice.....

Trixie bawled.

She went boneless.

She did everything she could to show how unhappy she was.

By the time they got home, her daddy was unhappy, too.

As soon as Trixie's mommy opened the door, she asked,

The whole family ran down the block.

They zoomed past the school,

and into the Laundromat.

But Knuffle Bunny was
nowhere to be found....

So Trixie's daddy
decided to look harder.

Until . . .

And those were the first words Trixie ever said.